How Wet Can

Adapted by Tish Rabe
from a script by Bruce Robb
Illustrated by Aristides Ruiz and Joe Mathieu

A Random House PICTUREBACK® Book

Random House 🏠 New York

Based in part on *The Cat in the Hat Knows a Lot About That!* TV series (Episode 12) © CITH Productions, Inc.
(a subsidiary of Portfolio Entertainment, Inc.), and Red Hat Animation, Ltd. (a subsidiary of Collingwood O'Hare Productions, Ltd.), 2010–2011.

THE CAT IN THE HAT KNOWS A LOT ABOUT THAT! logo and word mark TM 2010 Dr. Seuss Enterprises, L.P., Portfolio Entertainment, Inc.,
and Collingwood O'Hare Productions, Ltd. All rights reserved. The PBS KIDS logo is a registered trademark of PBS.
Both are used with permission. All rights reserved.

Broadcast in Canada by Treehouse™. Treehouse™ is a trademark of the Corus® Entertainment Inc. group of companies. All rights reserved.

Visit us on the Web!   Seussville.com   pbskids.org/catinthehat   treehousetv.com
Educators and librarians, for a variety of teaching tools, visit us at www.randomhouse.com/teachers
ISBN: 978-0-375-86517-6   Library of Congress Control Number: 2009943006
Printed in the United States of America
10 9 8 7 6 5 4 3 2 1

"When it rains," Sally said,
"it's fun to get wet!"
"Let's see," laughed Nick,
"just how wet we can get!

"Let's jump in this puddle!"
When Sally said "Yes!"
they jumped in and soon were . . .

. . . a mud-covered mess!

Then the Thinga-ma-jigger
flew in and—*ker-splat!*—
mud splashed all over
the Cat in the Hat!

"We're a mess!" Sally said.
"We need to get clean."
"Yes," said the Cat.
"I can see what you mean.

"We'll go on a trip,
and I will show you
how to get clean
like the animals do!"

"Here's Carol the sparrow.
She knows a few things
about getting dirt off of
her body and wings."

"First," said the sparrow,
"to get clean you must
cover yourself in a
shower of dust.

"Then flap your wings
to get dirt off of you.
It works for us birds.
It will work for you, too!"

"I like flapping," said Nick,
"but I really don't see—
if we're covered in dust,
just how clean can we be?"

"Don't worry!" the Cat said.
"Next we'll meet some cats
who clean with their tongues
and do not wear hats.

"Meet Leona the Lion.
When she licks her fur,
her tongue is so rough
it takes dirt right off her."

"That tickles!" laughed Sally.
"Their tongues do feel rough,
but to get a kid clean
I don't think that's enough."

"Hanna Hippo," the Cat said,
"will show us the way
she gets mud and bugs off
her skin every day."

"Join me," said Hanna,
"in this muddy pool.
I don't get clean here.
I just try to keep cool.

"I get clean when my friends
the oxpeckers begin
to peck all the mud
and the bugs off my skin."

So the oxpeckers started
their mud-pecking trick
and tried getting mud
off Sally and Nick.

"You know, Cat," said Nick,
"I never have heard
of a kid getting clean
with the help of a bird."

"You're right," said the Cat.
"And I think that it's time
to rid ourselves now
of this dirt and this grime."

"Hippos use birds to
keep mud from sticking.
Lions use tongues to
get clean by licking.

"Sparrows use dust to get
their feathers clean.
But we need something else
that we still haven't seen."

"I know!" said Sally.
"Let's hurry home now.
There's a way to get clean
and I'll show you how!

"We won't stand in a shower
or soak in a tub.
We won't need any soap
or a washcloth to scrub.

". . . a sprinkler!

"When we turn it on,
in just a few minutes
the mud will be gone!"